I am Raven

A Story of Discovery

David Bouchard & Andy Everson

MORE THAN WORDS
MTW
PUBLISHERS

To discover your totem is to discover yourself.

There are as many totems as there are species of birds, beasts or fish. And how not?
Are we not all different?

I am often asked how people come to know their totems. When
I am, I answer by asking this question: "If at night, when you close
your eyes to travel to your dream time, if then you picture
one of our wild cousins to whom you might give thanks or
ask guidance, what would it be?" More often than not,
your totem will be there, right before your eyes.
You do not have to get fancy, just close your
eyes and let it come to you. Chances are it will.
It did for me.

Some will tell you that your totem is something you were in a previous life or something you might become in the next. That might be true. Others will tell you that your totem is the source of your strengths and weaknesses. *This* I believe to be true. Understanding my totem helps me to understand myself. And when I come to know someone else's totem, it helps me better understand that person.

You do not have to know what your totem is to have one. You just do. You do not choose your totem. It chooses you. And you do not have to acknowledge it or celebrate its presence, but you can and when you do, it is good. The Creator blesses us all with an animal medicine spirit guardian to watch over, teach and guide us on our journeys through life. Understanding these totems helps us choose which path to take on that journey.

This story might help you come to know your totem. My Grandmother gave it to me. I am not giving it to you. I am merely telling it to you. You can share it only if someone asks you this question; "What is *my* totem?" If someone asks you this question, then you can tell them this story. And tell them that my Grandmother gave it to me, so it is true.

A great chief lived over there, somewhere to the west of here. My Grandmother told me his name and although I have forgotten what it is, his spirit still lives in my heart.

This chief was not known because he was a rich man, though he was said to be rich. He was known because he was kind and wise.

People from the north, east and south of this place came to him for counsel. Animals, birds and fish also sought out his counsel so you can imagine just how wise he must have been.

One day this chief decided to erect a new totem pole. He invited a number of our wild cousins to his lodge. Many came, but some did not. They had their reasons.

As custom dictates and as should always be done, they honoured their grandmothers and their grandfathers. They had tea. Then, the chief spoke. "Friends, I shall soon journey to the land of my ancestors. I want my descendants to remember me for who I am so I am having a pole carved. I cannot include all of you on this pole however I want you to know that you are all special to me."

Later that day, as he stepped out of his lodge, the chief saw Beaver next to a most beautiful canoe. "Oh hello Good Chief," Beaver said. "What are *you* doing here?"

The chief looked around, baffled. "What are you talking about Beaver? I live here! This is my lodge! *You* know that!"

"I suppose I do, however this is not important, is it?" continued Beaver. "Me? I was just passing by. Chief, I . . . I . . . would never want to influence your decision as to whom you will place on your pole, however, I built this canoe for you some time ago . . . and . . . well . . . I thought . . . Chief, you know me. I am the builder. I do not waste my time playing or dreaming like many of these others. From dawn to dusk, I work hard. With persistence and determination I create, much as you do. Look at what you have built here. This village was poor and run down. Today it stands as an example of what can be. Your legacy will surely be that of the builder!"

As he did every evening, the chief went for an evening walk and as he stepped onto a much used path he heard a familiar voice.

"My! My! My! What a surprise to find *you* out here in the wilderness this way my old friend! And just as I was about to bring you this important gift."

"Wilderness?" the chief laughed. "Bear! What are you talking about? We use this path as much as we use the sea and the rivers."

"Let us not argue over trivialities," Bear persisted. "The fact is I am happy to see you. I have something for you my friend. It is time I pass this ceremonial headpiece on to one who is wise and a natural born teacher. This ancestral piece must reside with one who is knowing, humble and strong. My spirit medicine has provided you and your human ancestors with the ability to heal your sick, your children and your elderly. Whoever wears this headdress will be given this ability to train others in my guardian medicine; to protect, heal and guide all those in need on their spiritual quest as they travel the Good Red Road. May you be blessed as you pass this healing medicine on."

The chief spent that entire evening accepting gifts.

First, he met Wolf returning from a successful hunt. Wolf, it seemed, had more meat than he could possibly eat and was only too happy to gift the better half of a tasty young buck to his life-long friend. "I am happy to share this meal with you Great Chief. After all, as well as being courageous and resourceful, do we not, you and I, protect our people and provide for them? Finding, then sharing a meal is what we do. I have always respected and shared with you two-leggeds. Honouring my spirit will bring increasing joy, laughter and prosperity to your people. Please my friend, eat well."

Next, he happened onto Owl. "I am delighted to run into you Good Chief and just in case I did, I brought this new medicine bag along with me. While in your lodge earlier today, I could not help but notice that yours was looking a little worse for wear."

"Chief, you know that I frighten those who see me as "one who can see into the dark side." But I am more than that. Those of us with this power find deep truth and we guide the young and the elders towards greater knowing and identity with the Creator. We should have a special place in which to keep the things we value most. Please, think of me as you wear this. It will help you remember 'who-who' you really are."

Eagle's gift was a traditional fan of his finest feathers. "My feathers are highly valued by all Nations and my down is a symbol of peace and friendship. We are always, you and I, honest and open because we are close to the Creator. Are these not the traits for which you wish to be remembered?"

The chief found Frog sitting on a large leaf. "I know you will not let yourself succumb to these material things, Great Leader. You and I understand that peace of mind and heart is key to happiness. The way in which we value our families and that which we carry in our hearts will be remembered long after either of us enters the spirit world. Please accept this tobacco and this sweet grass braid as a reminder of the quiet moments of reflection we have shared together. Consider these a token of the respect I have for you."

Killer whale waited. "Ah Chief . . . I see that I am not the first to reach you. I too believe that much of what you are is of me. You and I, we rule our respective domains; you these lands, and I, the oceans. We are communicators. Through us comes the history of all that has passed before us as well as the ability to share this wisdom. We gift our descendants the ability to co-create new peace, harmony and friendship with All Our Relations and our Mother the Earth. Please accept this talking stick as a reminder of that which we share."

Otter, who rarely stopped playing for anyone or anything, came bounding out of the river. "Thank the Creator for fun and games! What would life be without play? Has not our curiosity, yours and mine Great Chief, made our lives exciting and fun! I cannot believe how much you remind me of me. HO HAH! Look what I have been saving for you . . . new gaming sticks. HEY? Are you up for a little gaming right now?"

As Otter presented his gift, Thunderbird blinked and lightning danced across the skies. Thunder echoed from sea to sea as "he who commands the elements" flapped his mighty wings and lit up the mountains. "Most fear me for my power and my wrath. I am the Creator's message carrier so how could it not be so? Worthy friend, with my own hands, I have made you this most powerful spear, symbolic of the Creator's blessing to you for a life honouring all creatures. Use it as you will during your final hunts. Let all come to know of the friendship that exists between us!"

Though it was late, the chief made his way to a clearing near the water's edge. There sat Raven, unusually quiet.

"There you are, Raven. I am surprised I have not run into you this evening. Did you not have something you wanted to gift me? I have received many wonderful things this evening, but from you, nothing?"

Raven smiled. "Come over here. Look into the water and tell me what you see."

This chief looked down at what should have been his reflection only to see that of Raven. "What trick is this you are playing on me, Raven?"

"This is no trick Chief. It is as you see it. It is said that I am the trickster; the magician. And it is true. I am said to be intelligent and cunning. This is also true. It is said that I can make things happen that others cannot. This, of course, is true. By using the gifts the Creator has given me, I succeed where others fail. Does this not sound familiar to you?"

"Great Chief, I am your totem. I have taught you to look within yourself when you were confronted by new and difficult challenges. I have taught you to use your wit and your strengths to survive and thrive. And you have been masterful. No, I bring you no gift. All I have, I have already given you. All I am, you have become. And you, my friend, have made me proud to be Raven."

The next day, everyone came to a great potlatch to feast this chief's new pole. They were all given many gifts. They sang and danced and marveled at the way in which the chief would be forever remembered.

And no, none were surprised at what they saw. They *all* knew.

You too would know *your* totem if, before traveling to your dream time, you would shut your eyes, open your heart, mind and spirit, and let it come to you. Do not get fancy. Just shut your eyes. It will come. It did for me.

And Further Honouring . . .

This story is meant to start you on a journey of discovery. I have used the word "totem" to describe "animal spirit guardians." It should be noted that totems are something quite different from animal spirit guardians and that totems are not a gift from the creator. Totems are passed down through family lines. Recently, the term "totem" has been often and loosely used to describe animal spirit guides. I hope you will understand.

The totems I have included in my telling may or may not be you. There are so many. If you are to come to know those who guide you and who can help you through certain stages of your life, you might have to keep looking. You should learn to call on any number of spirit guides. Learn to make several your own.

I am a Raven; however I often call on other totems for strength and guidance. For example, when I am asked to teach, I carry the claw of Bear on my person. I do this as a reminder that I want to teach. I do not want to trick, which is of course how we Ravens tend to do things. I want to teach. I carry that claw in a medicine bag I hang around my neck. It is good to carry a fetish as a reminder of what we are and what we want to be.

The totems in this story are all strong and good but if you are to come to know the fullness of spirit guardians, you might want to continue along this path of discovery. The internet is a good place to look and there are many books available on totems. Talk to Elders and to people who know of such matters. Remember however, that the best place to look is always within yourself.

In this story, this chief could not include everyone on his pole; nor could I in my telling. I am particularly sorry to a few I did not include.

HUMMINGBIRD: You are perfect joy and love, a great beauty; and the messenger of things spiritual. Over time you always bring good fortune to those you guide. You are deliberate and gentle and have the most amazing stamina.

DUCK: You are nurturing and protective; you bring emotional comfort, grace and protection. You always find some way to make your dreams come true. You are resourceful and a most patient teacher. You insist on order and harmony in all things especially in families and communities. It is good that you are attentive to the needs and wants of others otherwise you would be hard to live with.

DRAGONFLY: If Dragons existed today, you might well be a Dragon. You are a thing of fairy tales; mystic and magic, and always your best in the sun's rays. You bring the power of light to see through all illusions, and winds of change for wise transformation into the next stage of being. You are an ancient soul that grows and changes at every turn. And you tend to be territorial, needing your own space to survive and thrive. Dragonfly, you are a joy and a wonder to behold.

CANADA GOOSE: You mate for life and have an intense emotional bonding with those you love. And you love to travel, both in spirit and in body. This yearning can sometimes pose you problems because there is so much to see and do in life. Fortunately, because you are so adept at teamwork, you always manage to achieve your goal. You are the inner spirit child in each of us that keeps us strong on our quest and life path, always full of wonder and stardust for our own unfolding.

When you start out on a journey, others should get out of your way. You love a mission and you undertake everything in life with determination and passion. Goose, have you ever noticed that your cry is what two-leggeds use to tell others to get out of their way? Cars do not cry out bow wow or tweet tweet. They call out HONK HONK!

SWAN: You are beauty, strength and love. You are poet, mystic and dreamer. You are blessed with powerful wings and a ferocious bite yet it is your pure and endless love that makes you what you are. In many civilizations, you are everything perfect. Great leaders are said to be of you. You are the ideal parent and the perfect mate and in my personal life, your love and nurturing has made you the perfect big sister.

LOON: You are solitude; one who re-awakens old dreams and those not yet dreamed. You are imaginative, independent, and you bring harmony to those you serve. You can lead others back to their dreams and imaginings. And your call . . . oh, your call is haunting. The challenge for you is to maintain balance between what you dream and the song you sing. That song is sometimes misunderstood because it lingers on calm waters and rests in troubled hearts. But you know that. You have dreamed it.

KINGFISHER: You are the promise of abundance, new warmth and prosperity. You love to be near the water. You are courageous, not afraid to take a chance. You love everything that is blue and are always ready to plunge into each and every endeavor, no matter how deep the water might seem; no matter how great the challenge might be. I have heard your song; WAI WAH (Just DO IT).

LADYBUG; You are sweet. You are gentle. You are inquisitive and always ready to help others. There is not a garden better served than the one you choose to inhabit. There is not a life not made richer than one that shares your company. You are devoted and loyal and have to watch out that others do not take advantage of your giving.

BEETLE: You are transformation. You move from east to west along the earth; nothing flighty for you. You are grounded and in almost every civilization, known as rebirth. You insist on rejuvenating some aspect of life, both your own and the lives of others. And you can always be counted on to show the path toward rejuvenation. You can be trusted. You are reliable. You are a survivor. You have always been. You will always be.

MOON: You are the guardian of your people's traditions (I constantly work at becoming Moon). You are spiritual, serene and wise, even at a young age. We love to look at you because you emanate an inner peace within us all. The thirteen Grandmothers have seen to this. Everyone can look to you for guidance. We should learn to share our challenges, concerns and successes with you. You are the perfect listener, always there for those who seek you out.

SUN: You are the source of inspiration and energy; the guiding light. You are the force of life and represent in us all growth and power. It took me time to recognize your presence within me, however over time, I have found you. Today, I recognize and celebrate your presence in me. I welcome you in my every activity. *I am Raven* came to me from you, Sun, my Nokum (Grandmother).

For Hagrid, my beautiful Irish wolfhound who is waiting for me in the Spirit World. Over his short lifetime, my loving friend taught me the fullness of unconditional love. He will always live in my heart and in the pages of this book.

— D.B.

For my Grandmother, Margaret Frank, who succeeded in living up to her Kwak'wala name, U'magalis. Through her 99 years of life she saw many changes, but was determined throughout that her culture live on. She instilled in me a profound belief in my traditions and taught me to be very proud of where I come from. Thank you Audie!

— A.E.

Copyright © 2007 David Bouchard
Art copyright © 2007 Andy Everson
First edition printed in Canada in 2007
This edition printed in Canada in 2009
5 4 3

LIBRARY AND ARCHIVES CANADA CATALOGUING IN PUBLICATION
Bouchard, David, 1952–
I am raven: a story of discovery / David Bouchard; illustrator, Andy Everson.
ISBN 978-0-9784327-0-6
1. Ravens – Fiction. I. Everson, Andy II. Title.
PS8553.O759I2 2007   C813'.54   C2007-904195-7

MTW Publishers
823 Hendecourt Road, North Vancouver, BC, Canada V7K 2X5
604.985.2527
www.mtwpublishers.com

David Bouchard *www.davidbouchard.com*
Andy Everson *www.andyeverson.com*

Editorial support by Bonnie Chapman and Joseph Martin
Copyedited by Bonnie Chapman
Book design by Arifin Graham, Alaris Design
Printed and bound in Canada by Friesens on 10% pcw recycled paper ✫